WELCOME HOME, HENRY

HOLT, RINEHART AND WINSTON, INC. New York, Toronto, London, Sydney

A Monkeying-Around-With-Print Book

a Bill Martin Instant Reader

# WELCOME HOME, HENRY

by Bill Martin, Jr. with pictures by Muriel Batherman

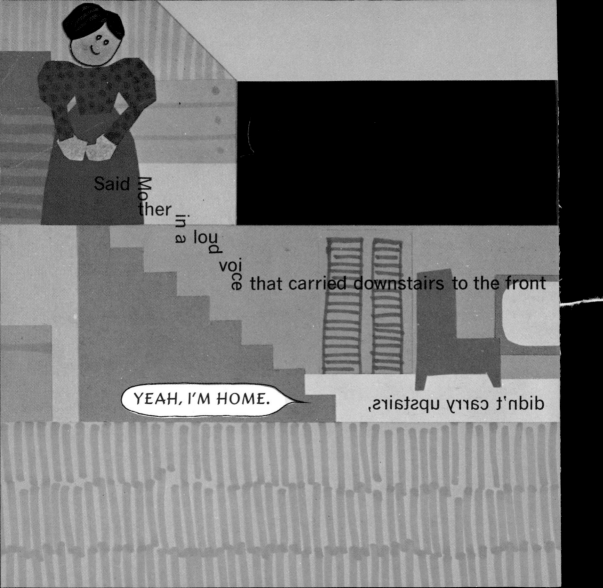

Said Mother in a loud voice that carried downstairs to the front

didn't carry upstairs,

YEAH, I'M HOME.

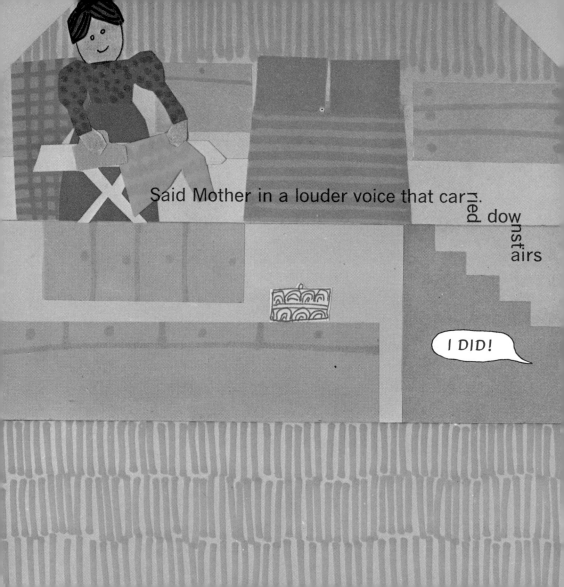

Said Mother in a louder voice that carried downstairs

I DID!

Said Mother in her loudest voice that carried.

NO, I'M NOT.

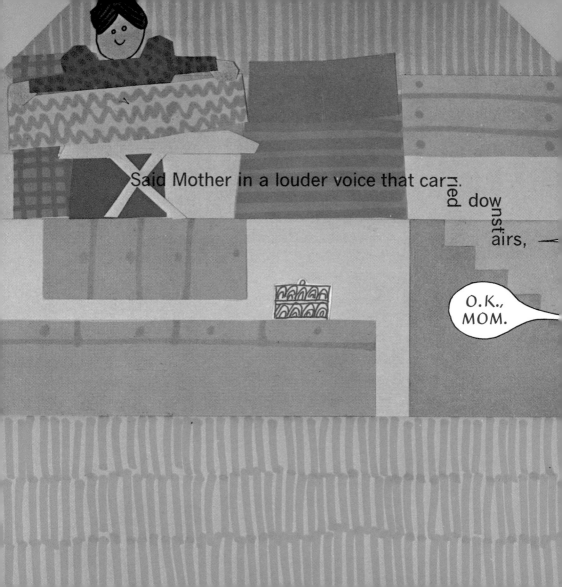

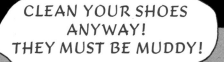

CLEAN YOUR SHOES
ANYWAY!
THEY MUST BE MUDDY!

Said Henry in a quiet voice that

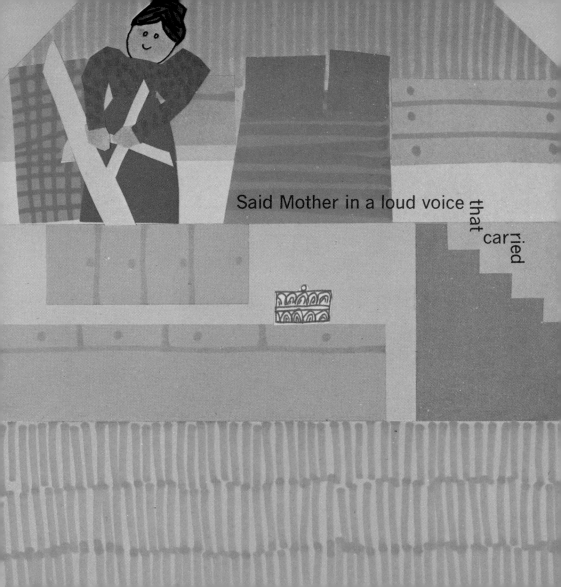

Said Mother in a loud voice that carried.

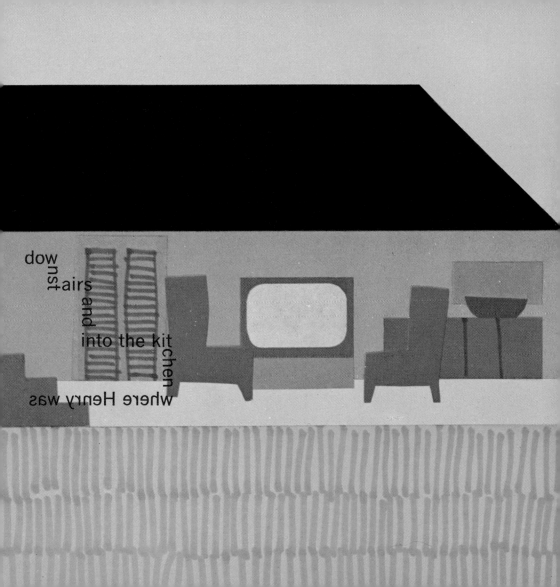

dow
nst
airs
and
into the kit
chen
where Henry was

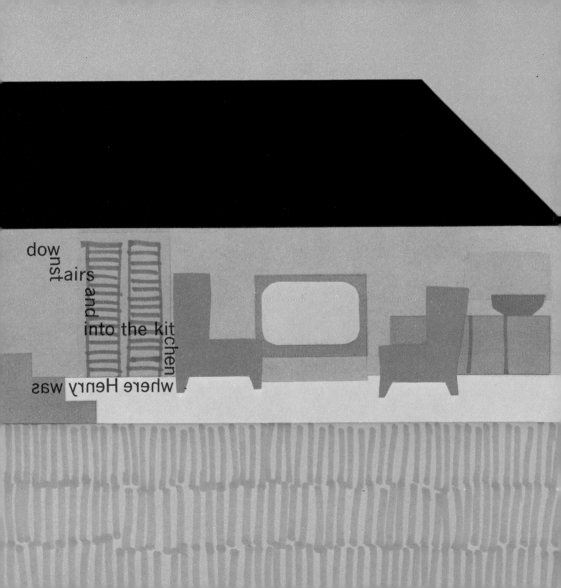

down
nst
airs
and
into the kit
chen
where Henry was

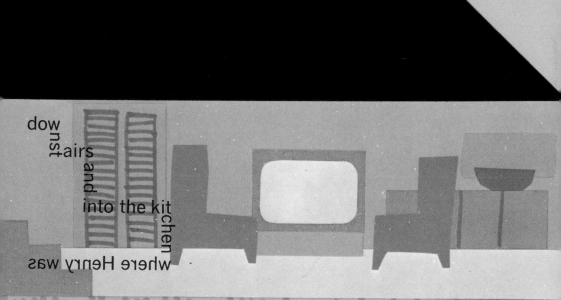

down
nst
airs
and
into the kit
chen
where Henry was

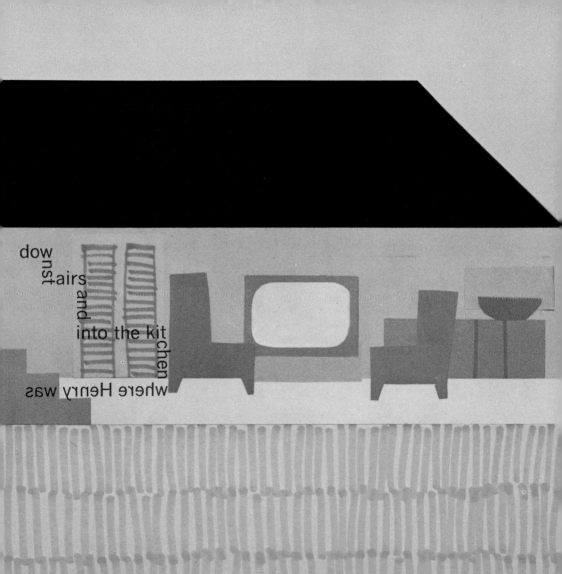

downstairs and into the kitchen where Henry was

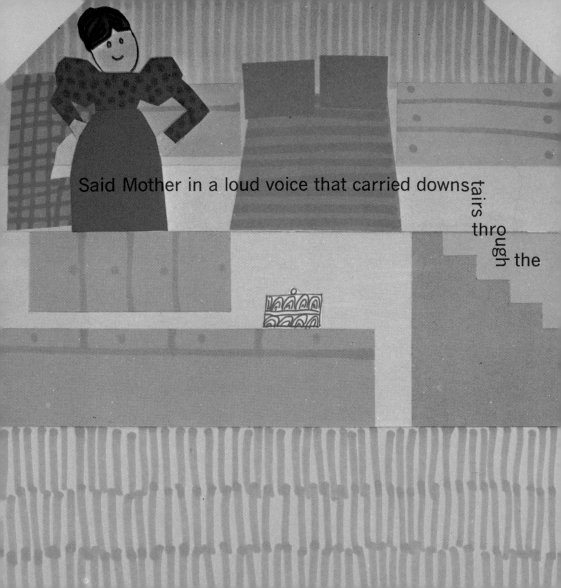

Said Mother in a loud voice that carried downstairs through the

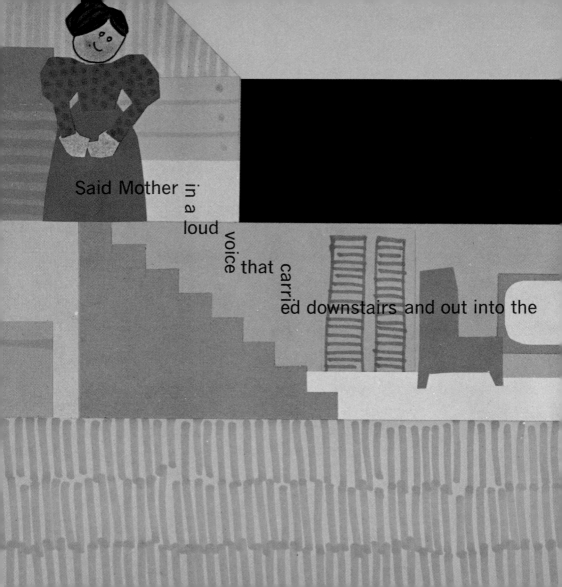

Said Mother in a loud voice that carried downstairs and out into the